THE CAT AND
THE RIVER THAMES

The Adventures of Boathouse Mouse

Book 2

THE CAT AND
THE RIVER THAMES

Written by RU Hodge
Pictures by Shawna Apps

Dedicated to every child who would like to have a boating adventure.
- RV Hodge

For Gordon and Melanie
For always encouraging me to follow
my dreams when I grew up.
- Shawna Apps

Dear Mother and Father,

I sure miss you both and the rest of the family.

I am really enjoying the ship life even though it can be hard work. Every day there is some new adventure or something amazing to learn. So far I have seen many other ships at sea. I had no idea there were so many. I've watched dolphins swimming and jumping. Their acrobatics are very entertaining. We had a pod of whales near us for part of one day. They are huge and, as odd as it sounds, they breathe through a hole on top of their head. It is really loud when you are close. Sometimes they spray water out too. That looks kind of funny. And I saw some curious-looking little fish with wings. The sailors called them flying fish.

All last week we were battered by a terrible storm. It was very scary and I was seasick at first. I learned from the sailors to nibble my food a little bit at a time so I always had something in my tummy. That made the seasickness better, but I still do not like storms at sea. I'm glad that one is over. *Wanderer* performed flawlessly, and Captain Banderas is an excellent captain. He always knows what to do.

One of our longboats broke loose from its davits and got damaged during the storm. I'm sure I'll be busy helping the ship's carpenter repair it. I don't know where we will work, as there is no shop on board the ship.

I have a little time to write now because we are at anchor. Last night we got too close to the shores of an island called Guernsey, so we have to wait until the tide turns. The shoreline is rugged and the sea crashes on the rocks with frightening sounds. The sea air smells like kelp here, and it is cold. Wait, Captain Banderas has given the order to weigh the anchor. There is a lot of activity on the deck. I just felt the ship move as the anchor broke free from the bottom. We are under way again! In three days, I will be in London, England!

Love to all,
Boathouse Mouse

As *Wanderer* sailed up the River Thames, Boathouse Mouse watched in awe from his favorite scupper. The city of London came slowly into view, and Boathouse was surprised at how smoky the city was.

When *Wanderer* was made fast to the stanchions on the dock, the sailors prepared to offload their cargo. There was a general air of excitement as the sailors anticipated the change in activity and a day off in the city.

Boathouse helped the ship's carpenter untie the longboat so it could be repaired. He was inside the boat when it was hoisted off the ship onto a wagon that was marked Greenwich Bend Boat Shop. Boathouse was surprised and wondered, *Where are we going?* Suddenly the cart began moving and Boathouse had no choice but to go along. In minutes, he was entranced by the bustling city full of strange sights.

They rolled past building after building. Some were so large they seemed to reach the clouds. He was amazed by a huge clock tower that was visible for miles. They passed a regal-looking palace with stern-faced guards. Everywhere he looked there were new buildings being built and old buildings being torn down.

Eventually they crossed a bridge and the town began to look older and rougher. They passed through a smelly fish market with more stray cats than Boathouse ever imagined existed. With his heart racing, he ducked into the boat so they could not see him.

Then the wagon bounced along a country lane that had farms with small cottages. Boathouse saw pastures full of cows and sheep. He even saw an old man using a dog to herd sheep from one pasture to another.

Presently the wagon was backed into a shed, and the longboat was hoisted onto some sawhorses. When everything got quiet, Boathouse crept out and looked around. He was amazed to see so many familiar tools. The shop was smaller, but much like the one he was raised in.

Suddenly a voice called to him, "Hey there, mate, did you ride in on that boat?"

Boathouse jumped in alarm. He was about to run when he saw a mouse in blue overalls holding tools. Boathouse stammered, "Who are you?"

"Catspaw is the name. But most folks call me Cat. And who might you be?" the mouse replied with a thick accent.

"I'm Boathouse Mouse," Boathouse returned. "How ever did you get a name like that?"

Cat held up a curved pry bar. "I guess I use the cat's paw more than anyone else in the shop. And how did a ship's mouse get a name like Boathouse?"

"I was raised in a boathouse building a ship. When it was finished, I took a job on the ship to seek adventure," Boathouse explained proudly.

Cat looked him over and exclaimed, "Pleasure to meet you, Boathouse! Now be a mate and grab a mallet. There's jolly plenty of nails to unclinch before we can get these brutalized planks unmounted. We've not got but ten days to have this little gem back to the *Wanderer*."

"You know about *Wanderer*?" Boathouse asked in amazement as he grabbed a hammer and helped Cat.

"Course I do, mate, she's right across the way there." Cat pointed out the door.

Boathouse looked, and there was his proud ship, directly across the River Thames, tied up to the docks. He could see the sailors busily hoisting out the cargo.

Cat said, "She's a beaut!"

"Yes, she is." Boathouse swelled with pride. "I built her."

Cat asked, "Single-handedly?"

Boathouse replied, "Yep, just me and about two dozen shipwrights."

"Two dozen!" Cat exclaimed. "How did you ever stay out of sight with so many? We've only got three here."

The two boat builders became great friends as they worked on the longboat. Boathouse found himself telling Cat sea stories like he was an old salt. Then, before they knew it, the boat repair was completed. Cat and Boathouse scurried off the boat before a boatwright began painting it. They did not want to be around the awful smell of the boat paint.

As they were enjoying scones and tea, Cat confessed, "You know, mate, I've always wondered what it would be like to ship off for an adventure."

Boathouse exclaimed, "Oh, you should ship on *Wanderer*! It would be fun, and we could see the whole world!"

"I'm not so sure I would like it," Cat hesitated. "My family is all here, and I've got a great job and all. Maybe I could get a tour of the ship and then decide?"

"I'll be glad to give you a tour of my ship. I'm sure you will like it," Boathouse replied. "Be sure to pack your things."

The next morning Boathouse Mouse and Catspaw Mouse were stowed away on the longboat as it was rowed across the river to the ship. There was a thump as the longboat came alongside the ship, and in a few minutes the newly repaired boat was hoisted up to its place. The two adventurers slipped to the ship's deck. Boathouse gave Cat the grand tour from one end of *Wanderer* to the other.

Cat was awestruck. "This is amazing! How long will the voyage be before the ship returns to London?"

Boathouse thought about the upcoming ports of call he had heard the captain speak about. "I don't think we'll be back to London for a long time. Maybe a few years," Boathouse replied.

Catspaw was quiet for a few minutes as he looked across the river at the Greenwich Bend Boat Shop. Finally he decided, "I can't be gone for so long, mate. My family needs me here. Good ventures to you, my friend Boathouse." Then he scampered to catch a ride across the river.

Boathouse waved goodbye to his friend from his favorite scupper. He was happy to be back on his ship, but sad to leave his friend behind.

Boathouse went to the cargo holds to see what had been loaded on the ship. There were hundreds of rolls of deep blue cotton fabric. *Where are we taking all this cloth?* he wondered, and hurried up to the captain's quarters to see the great map. He followed the traced lines from London back out to the Atlantic Ocean, then around into the Mediterranean Sea. The charted lines ended at Constantinople, Turkey.

Constantinople, Turkey. The very name sounded exotic. Boathouse was almost too excited to fall asleep that night.

Something in the middle of the night woke Boathouse. He listened, but could not hear anything that sounded wrong. He grabbed his toolbox and went to the deck to inspect for any damage, but found none, only one night watchman snoring against a coil of rope.

Suddenly a motion caught his attention, and Boathouse looked down the aft dock line. Rats! There were a lot of rats and they were coming up the line. Boathouse was terrified! They were much larger than he was, but he did not know how to wake the watchman. He knew rats could not be allowed to board the ship, so he grabbed his hammer and jumped onto the dock line. "You may not board this ship!" Boathouse called out.

The lead rat stopped and all the others stopped behind him. The lead rat had a ring in one ear and wore a sword like he knew how to use it. He sneered, "I'll board any ship I decide to. I've got an army, and they'll throw you overboard, little mouse!"

"You have to fight me before your army can get on this ship!" Boathouse proclaimed with confidence he did not feel.

"Then I'll throw you overboard myself," the lead rat threatened, and stepped closer to Boathouse.

"Without me, the ship will sink," Boathouse stated calmly.

With that, one of the rats in the back cried out, "Sinking ship! Abandon ship! We're going down!"

Many of the rats panicked and tried to crowd down the line at the same time. The lead rat turned around and shouted back, "Stay in formation, you imbeciles! The ship is not SINKING!"

Most of the rest of the rat army only heard the word "sinking," and that was all it took. The terrified rats jumped into the water and swam for shore.

The leader was left with only two of his followers. As he turned back to face Boathouse, he drew his sword. Boathouse was very afraid, but he held up his hammer because he had no idea what else to do. To Boathouse's astonishment, the three rats suddenly turned and ran down the rope as fast as rats can run.

Relief swept over Boathouse and, as he stepped off the line, he all but bumped into a cat. He instantly realized that the cat had scared the last three rats. He also realized there was nowhere to run.

The cat said, "That was remarkable. I've never met a mouse with such courage."

Boathouse stammered, "Does that mean you're not going to eat me?"

The cat looked insulted. "Eat you? Do I look like some mongrel alley cat? Great guns, what kind of pathetic tub have I been dumped onto? Six years' faithful service on the queen's finest man-o-war and, with one pirate's musket ball to the hip, I'm reduced to ... to this!"

"This is not a tub! Not pathetic!" Boathouse shook the hammer like a pointer at the cat. "This is a civilized merchant ship, made to the highest modern standards of ship building. And ... it is commanded by none other than Captain Banderas himself!"

The cat looked at Boathouse with amusement. "Never heard of him," the cat replied.

Boathouse finished his tirade weakly, "And I built this ship."

The cat and mouse stared at each other for a long time, then the cat simply said, "The rats are coming back."

Boathouse looked down the dock line and saw the rats beginning to climb again. "I don't know what to do."

"I do," the cat responded. "Rule number one in battle: Always have a plan, and a backup. Now, I can either waste my life here, chasing smelly rats off the line, or ... "

Boathouse looked back to see why the cat had not finished his sentence. The cat was by the sleeping watchman. "You see that paddle near this snoring lout's hand?" The cat was pointing at a board. Boathouse nodded.
"That," the cat emphasized, "is supposed to be used to smack the line every quarter hour. It is simple and effective. Unfortunately, most guards fall asleep at two o'clock in the night watch." Then the cat casually bared his claws and stuck them deep into the sleeping watchman's leg.
The man howled with pain as he jumped up. "Gato idiota!" the guard exclaimed as he grabbed his paddle and began smacking the dock line energetically. The rats ran back to shore as predicted.

The cat rubbed against the sailor's leg, then stepped behind the coil of rope where Boathouse was hidden. "By the way, the name is Commodore Thomas."

"My name is Boathouse Mouse," Boathouse replied.

"My pleasure," the cat returned as they shook hands. "Let's go below. Maybe the cook has started something good for breakfast."

"Can I ride on your back when we engage pirates?" Boathouse requested.

"Umm, no!" the cat retorted.

"May I call you Tommy?" Boathouse asked.

The cat gave him a sidelong glance. "Absolutely not." He sniffed indignantly.

"How about Tom?" Boathouse queried.

"Must you?" the cat implored.

"It's much easier," Boathouse answered.

Tom sighed. They were both happy to have a friend.

Later that morning, as *Wanderer* was taking the first tide out to sea, Boathouse watched from his favorite scupper.

Tom said, "I thought I might find you here."

Boathouse jumped with surprise. "How did you know?" he asked.

"Well," the cat replied, "You're a boatbuilder, so you would know the best view. And this is one of the few scuppers that gives you someplace to stay hidden as you watch."

Boathouse nodded, then questioned, "I've noticed you have a limp. Is that from the musket ball?"

Tom answered, "Yes, but some things are not polite to ask about."

Boathouse did not take the hint. "So you were shot by a pirate?"

The cat looked out the scupper and answered elusively, "It was a long time ago, and the details are a bit fuzzy now."

Boathouse's imagination was running wild. "Did the pirates know you were a fearsome foe? Did you see the man who fired on you? Did you have to take care of the wound by yourself? Were you decorated as a hero?"

Commodore Thomas sat down beside Boathouse and, with a deep sigh, said, "Okay, kid, here's the deal. The battle was over and I was running to retrieve the feather that had blown out of the captain's hat. I slipped on a slick spot and landed on this random musket ball that was rolling around on the deck, right on the hip. It did hurt pretty bad then. But over the years, it's kind of gotten arthritic and it slows me down. That's no good for a battleship cat, so I got retired."

Boathouse looked at his new friend and replied, "I won't mention it again."

Tom asked, "So, where are we headed?"

"Constantinople," Boathouse replied.

"Ah, you'll love Turkey. Very colorful, and the food is extraordinary," Tom said.

"Pirates?" Boathouse asked with concern.

"Not likely," Tom replied.

As the River Thames opened up into the sea, the two friends watched in anticipation of their next adventure.

CPSIA information can be obtained
at www.ICGtesting.com
Printed in the USA
BVOW07s0018120716

455186BV00006B/12/P